This igloo book belongs to:

....

D0538181

igloobooks

Published in 2019
by Igloo Books Ltd
Cottage Farm
Sywell
NN6 0BJ
www.igloobooks.com

Copyright © 2015 Igloo Books Ltd
Igloo Books is an imprint of Bonnier Books UK

1219 003
4 6 8 10 9 7 5 3
ISBN 978-1-78905-663-1

Written by Melanie Joyce
Illustrated by Gabi Murphy

Cover designed by Lee Italiano
Interiors designed by Jason Shortland
Edited by Natalia Boileau

Printed and manufactured in China

Make Me Smile

igloobooks

I love you all the way from your head to your toes.

I even love your ears
and your big, swishy nose.

You make me smile when you
pull funny faces.

I always laugh at your
strange hiding places.

Sometimes you are grumpy,
but you are also very kind.

I know that you love me,
so I really don't mind.

It makes me smile when
you mess around.

You giggle and make
a trumpeting sound.

When you start dancing,
you boogie on by.

It looks so funny,
I laugh till I cry.

You make me smile with
such fun things to eat.

There's always some
yummy, delicious treat.

You tell brilliant tales
and act them out, too.

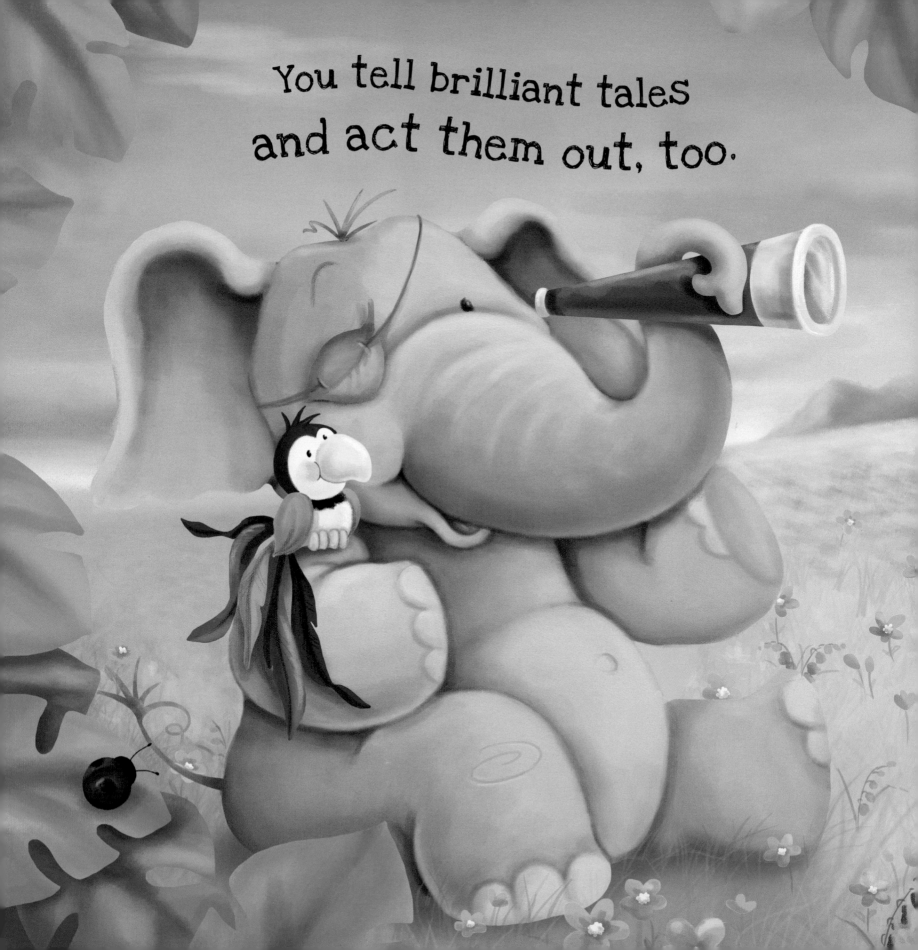

No one does storytime
quite like you do.

I love it when my
friends come to play.

You join in our games
and we have fun all day.

You make me smile
in stormy weather.

I feel so safe when
we are huddled together.

At bedtime you stay
with me for a while.

I dream of you and how you make me smile.